A
Sudden
Elegance

A
Sudden
Elegance

Iridescent Toad Publishing

Iridescent Toad Publishing.

Cover art by DLR Cover Designs.

First edition. ISBN 978-1-913779-33-7

Chapter One

It was a cold winter's day in the South East of Queen Victoria's England. The ice was thin on the ground as the small horse-drawn carriage swayed tentatively against the lack of traction. Christmas had recently passed, and as hard as the year gone by had been, the people had welcomed the beauty of the snowfall – the rich people who could afford the means to cope with the freezing temperatures, blustering winds and unforgiving snowfall, that is.

Roberta Clancy cuddled her wool shawl tightly around her small but strong frame. She had been given it as a parting gift from her previous owners – a generous present considering the difficult situation that they had found themselves in. Roberta had served as a maid to the husband and wife since she'd turned fourteen. Just six years later, they had fallen on hard times and as a result, they had needed to sell many of their assets as well as their servants, one of whom was

Roberta. And so here she found herself being transported to her new home. She didn't know what to expect, only that it would probably take some getting used to.

Her now previous master and mistress had been sad to see her go. The mistress in particular had taken great care to explain the situation honestly to Roberta. Roberta was grateful for the fact that she hadn't found out that she would be serving somewhere else through the grapevine of gossip that could make its way so easily around the servant quarters. The mistress must have felt guilty about having to let her go because she had even invited Roberta to sit with her over a cup of tea as she explained everything to her. Roberta was to go to a new owner out in the country and, as the mistress saw it, it would be a considerable change of pace compared to life in the city. The markets wouldn't be as local, if at all, and new and unfamiliar rural duties might be the order of the day in her new placement.

Roberta was sad to leave her old employers. They had always treated her well. It was hard work but they had always been fair with her and she had never felt fearful of them. She respected them both as the heads of the house and the dynamic had always felt comfortable. She had seen a few other servants come and go in the time she was there; mainly because they weren't as keen on the hard work as she was, and had a tendency to answer back. Overall though, the main core of servants that had been there over a longer period of time had all taken a lot of pride in their work and got on well with each other. Getting up to peel potatoes and clean the stove was always hard but morale didn't seem to suffer when all of the servants got on and pulled their weight together.

Roberta sighed to herself, thinking about how much she was going to miss her old life. It had all happened so quickly and she hadn't expected to get a say in any of it. In that regard, she was right. For everything else though, the unknown was ahead. She was reminded of how cold it was as she saw her breath steam up right in front of her.

"It's going to be a bitter one tonight," said the coachman, his words echoing back to Roberta as the horses trotted tentatively down the country road. "I best be getting back straight away once you're there."

Roberta couldn't quite picture where "there" was and what it would look like. She had been born back in the town and had lived there all her life up until now. She wasn't uncomfortable with change overall. In fact, she considered herself to be very accommodating and adaptable. In the circumstances though, she couldn't help but feel anxious. The wind whipped at her cheeks and she felt the sting of it against them like tiny needles.

"I wish I knew where we were going," she shouted out to the coachman.

"It's just a few more miles," he informed her confidently. "It should only take another few hours."

"Even though you're not familiar with where we're going, can you tell me anything about it?"

The coachman chewed on his lower lip, concentrating to balance his thoughts with the demands of the icy road ahead.

"Well, based on what your new employer paid for you when the master and mistress had to auction off all their assets, I would hazard a guess that they're not too short when it comes to wealth. I get the impression that whoever purchased you put a fair bit of thought into it because they were offered the chance to purchase other servants but they only chose you. I guess they were either bowled over by your good references or they weren't in the market for more servants than they really need, not that you heard that from me of course."

The coachman smiled, seeming pleased with himself at being able to tell Roberta something new during what was a time of great uncertainty for her.

"Do you know who exactly made the purchase?" Roberta asked, ready to listen intently.

"I'm afraid that I don't know," said the coachman.

Roberta reasoned that she would have to take his word for it. He seemed honest enough. There had been very few occasions where she had interacted with him before because it was rare that she had left the master and mistress' house when in service to them. Her days had typically been spent attending to what they needed – usually cooking and cleaning. She sometimes used to envy the other maids when they went away for a couple of days each year to see their families. It wasn't that she hadn't been offered the same opportunity, it was that she had nowhere to go and nobody to see on account of having been orphaned not long before she had been granted the chance to work as a maid in her teens.

Roberta hadn't minded being indoors. It was predictable and everyone was nice enough. She'd felt that it was better than having to go to the workhouse. She had heard tales of others who had met such a fate and she was grateful that she had been offered an alternative. It meant that she had her own bed to sleep in.

Her mind wandered off to speculating on what her new living quarters would be like. Where would she sleep? Would she be able to eat when she was hungry? What would the other servants be like? And most of all, what would her new employer be like?

As the horses trotted onwards towards wherever it was that she was destined to go, she closed her eyes against the sleet that sprinkled against her pale skin. Hugging her shawl intensively as she shivered against the cold, she knew that she wouldn't have long to wait before her questions would be answered.

Chapter Two

Once the coachman had dropped Roberta off at the front of the estate, he hadn't waited around to see if everything would be ok. He wasn't obliged to do so and he was anxious to get back before the weather became any more intolerable than it already was. This left Roberta in a vulnerable situation.

It was pitch-black outside and the house was large. It had so many doors and windows and in being unfamiliar with it, Roberta had to creep around tentatively to assess how she might best be able to get access to the entrance.

Surely this must be the right place? she wondered to herself. There was nowhere else nearby, just a good few miles of fields.

The grass felt crisp underneath the soles of her shoes as Roberta figured that she must have missed the entrance to the house. She hadn't even managed to walk around the whole thing but knowing that it was getting colder and that surely someone must be expecting her, she reasoned that her safest bet was to ease her way back around to what she assumed was the front of the building where the coachman had dropped her off.

Roberta cursed herself for being so prone to over-thinking. One of the comforts she had always found in being in service was in knowing that someone else would always be making the decisions for her. An overactive mind like hers was not one to benefit from having too much freedom of choice. She knew it and she was very much at peace with it.

Her teeth continued to chatter away so violently that she feared she could bite through her tongue without realising it before it was too late. As her mind started to wander further into an abyss of abstract and uncomfortable thoughts, she noticed a flicker of orange light glowing through a small crack in the building.

As she walked closer towards it, she noticed a large door that had been left ajar. Under normal circumstances she wouldn't wish to be so brash as to storm inside uninvited, but these weren't normal circumstances. And so gently pushing the large wooden door with the icy tips of her fingers, she braced herself for whatever it was that she might find behind it.

The corridor behind the door was so eerily quiet that Roberta didn't dare to call out to see if anyone was there. She noted that – wherever this place was and whoever it belonged to – it was far grander than what she had grown used to at her last address.

The corridor had clearly been attended to recently because several candles had been lit. As the flames on them danced they created shadows that darted and flickered across the elaborately decorated walls and right up to the high ceilings. This drew Roberta's attention to the fact that she was spoilt for choice as to where to go next. The view before her was punctuated with numerous doors, most of which appeared to be locked. Not only that, but there were several staircases trailing off towards goodness knows how many parts of the house.

As she tried her best to take it all in, Roberta wondered how many other servants she would be working with at such a large house. On the one hand, she hoped that there would be many servants on the basis of how demanding the upkeep of such a place could be. On the other, she was anxious that within a large body of servants, it could take some time to get to know everyone and it could be hard to make friends. After all, it mattered to her not to feel alone in what would be her new home for the foreseeable, especially what with having been at her last address for so long.

As the enormity of the situation hit her, Roberta was keen to get someone's attention. She needed to find someone who could help her get settled in but equally, she didn't want to cause a disturbance. She would be mortified to do that on her first day!

"Hello," she whispered cautiously. "Is there anybody here?"

Nothing. No answer. Not a soul.

Luckily, just as Roberta had started to walk back towards the door through which she had entered the corridor, a voice – although flustered – chirped joyfully at her.

"Glad you found your way in. I left the door open for you so I hope you weren't out there for too long."

Startled, Roberta spun around to see who was talking to her. It was an older woman with a friendly round face. She continued to talk quickly at Roberta.

"We've been expecting you so I left the door open for you. I didn't know how long it would take me to get everything done upstairs and so rather than risk you getting cold outside, I guessed the kind thing to do would be to leave the door open. Usually I wouldn't want to gamble getting in trouble by letting a draught in, but you know, first impressions of new colleagues and all that..."

The woman bounded jovially towards Roberta and extended her calloused hand.

"My name's Jane. Nice to meet you."

"I'm Roberta."

"Let's get you inside and sorted. I am informed by Master Cutler that he's satisfied with your references. He's not in a rush to meet you, not at this hour anyway. He likes to have time to himself unless he wants a hot drink making."

"Is he the owner of this place?" Roberta asked,

struggling to take it all in. "Is *he* who you work for? Is he who *I* will be working for?"

"Yes, yes and yes," replied Jane, slightly amused and certainly endeared towards Roberta's wide-eyed curiosity.

Roberta cocked her head to one side, bemused at how Jane could be so upbeat this late in the day. *Maybe she just likes meeting new people,* Roberta thought to herself. She was snapped out of her reverie by Jane's enthusiasm.

"Right then," said Jane. "You look bloody freezing. Let's get you started so you can get warmed up."

And with that, Jane charged ahead further down the corridor, leaving Roberta to obediently follow along.

Chapter Three

Knowing that she and Roberta would have an early start ahead of them, Jane had wasted no time in escorting the new servant to where she would be staying. It was a small room with six beds. They were comfortable enough – not lavish, but comfortable. Roberta had expected to get some sleep that night but she was disappointed that she didn't manage to. As exhausted as she was from her journey, the anxiety of being in a new situation kept her awake. She appreciated how welcoming Jane had been but all the same, there would be lots of things to get used to in her new role. Roberta knew that she would need to keep her wits about her if she was going to be kept on by her new employer. Throughout her time in service, she had heard stories of servants who had been sent away and passed around. Sometimes they went somewhere that was an upgrade where the workload was easier and the living quarters were more comfortable. Often though, they ended up in a more arduous situation. Roberta hoped and prayed that in her new role – if the bed was anything to go by – she would be able to make a good impression on her new employer.

Jane didn't need to work hard to get Roberta's attention by the time it came to getting her out of bed for her first day.

"Roberta," she whispered. "Roberta… Oh!... You're already awake I see. I hope I didn't startle you."

"You didn't startle me. I didn't sleep well."

"Hey, don't feel bad about it," Jane said kindly. "I was exactly the same when I first got here. Honestly, don't worry about it. We've got a long day ahead of us and I know you'll get plenty of sleep tonight."

"Here's hoping," Roberta said doubtfully.

Roberta had always been such a worrier. She kept it together by reminding herself that how she was feeling was normal in the circumstances.

"Right then," said Jane clapping her hands together with enthusiasm. "Your clothes are over there on the side. We all wear the same uniform here. It makes it so much easier for washing because nobody has their own garments. Just grab whichever one you like off of the pile because they're all the same anyway. The master of the house likes us to present ourselves in a way that is clean and tidy. He takes a lot of pride in the appearance of his servants and you mustn't bring shame upon him – or us – with any tardiness. Equally though, it's important that you don't get the garment you're wearing so messy that you need to wash it all too often. With all the other work we have to do here, there simply isn't the time for it."

Roberta was surprised at Jane's enthusiasm considering the demanding nature of the work being described. Promptly walking towards the pile of garments so as not to insult Jane's efforts at seeming cheerful at this time of the morning, Roberta began to go through them. They were very dignified; long black dresses designed to cover the whole body from the neck to the ankles. To be worn with each dress was a pile of long white aprons and white bonnet hats.

Roberta hadn't had a uniform as such at her last place. All of the servants had pretty much worn what they'd arrived in and were provided with a new outfit once every few years when the situation warranted it. As a result, all of the servants at her last address had never matched each other in terms of dress. In comparison, everything felt so regimented now as she set about putting on her new uniform.

"Wear the shoes that you came in for now," instructed Jane. "These dresses are very forgiving and can hide a multitude of sins."

Roberta smiled as she finished tying her apron at the back.

"Anyway," Jane continued. "Take this apple for breakfast. You can eat it while I show you around."

Roberta felt strangely enchanted by Jane's lively approach. Not only was she endeared to it, but she appreciated it greatly. Maybe she would make a friend after all. That said though, Roberta cautiously reminded herself that maybe Jane was only being welcoming because she had a job to do. Besides, if Jane didn't do a good job of inducting a new servant, it would probably reflect badly on her. Roberta reasoned that self interest always came into play for people somewhere along the line.

Taking ravenous bites into the crisp green apple as Jane showed her around the house, Roberta struggled to take it all in; there was a lot to learn. There were so many different rooms and corridors that she was sure she would get lost. She started to worry that it would take her so long to find her way around that it could make her struggle to get things done in a timely manner, at least for a while into her new employment. Shaking her head determinedly, Roberta told herself that she needed to learn quickly. There could be no excuses. She was starting to think that her new employer would be quite grand and possibly as part of that, insistent. She hoped to herself that they would have the propensity to be forgiving if she made mistakes at first but at this stage, such a thing remained unknown.

After what seemed like a good hour or so, Roberta noticed how tired her legs were. As she stole a brief opportunity to bend down and rub them a little, Jane observed.

"And you've not seen the whole house yet… Or indeed the gardens. Or the farm. Or the courtyard."

"Wow!" said Roberta, surprised. "Just how big is this place? I've never seen anything like it!"

"Well, luckily for us, Master Cutler has so many servants that not everybody has to know – or indeed do – everything," said Jane reassuringly. "Speaking of which, this is his study and he should probably be in here at this time of the morning. If he is, it would be a good opportunity for you to meet him."

Chapter Four

No sooner had Jane moved forward to knock on the door of the study, she stopped dead in her tracks before her knuckles could come into contact with the wood. Swiftly, she motioned back to Roberta that they needed to make themselves unnoticeable. Roberta didn't need to ask why. It was evident from the commotion that could be heard from inside the study. It echoed distinctively through the walls; anyone in the corridor would have been able to hear it.

Drawing her finger to her pursed lips in a shushing motion, Jane signalled to Roberta to keep quiet and listen to the sounds that were coming from the study. It was the sound of a woman sobbing. Her sobs were occasionally punctuated with a man talking in a low voice. He sounded stern and angry. Every time the man said something, the sobbing from the woman seemed to increase.

"That's your new boss," Jane carefully mouthed to Roberta. "Master Cutler."

Roberta's heart sank. What kind of man could her new employer be if he made his servants cry like that? *So much for first impressions*, she thought to herself.

Jane and Roberta leaned in as far as they could towards the closed door to hear what was being said, but very little information was available to them until the door flew open and the sobbing maid ran out of the room crying hysterically.

The man who Roberta figured must be her new employer then stepped slowly out into the corridor. He looked calm enough but it was evident that just moments ago, something had been a major source of annoyance for him. Turning to Jane, with a strong extent of focus in his tone, the man instructed her.

"I need you to make arrangements for her departure from the premises. She will be carted off to work for someone else."

Saying nothing, Jane nodded compliantly.

The man ignored Roberta as he swept right past

her in a hurry to deal with something else that was clearly more of a pressing issue for him in that moment.

First impressions indeed! Roberta thought to herself.

28

Chapter Five

It wasn't long before Roberta found herself in the kitchen peeling potatoes. Jane had quickly got her started on it and had then left to deal with what Master Cutler had asked of her earlier.

Not wanting to pry but concerned about how the morning's events could potentially have an impact on her at some point, Roberta cautiously questioned Jane.

"So what was that all about?"

"Well, between you and me, it ain't pretty," Jane said candidly.

"Oh?" said Roberta, trying to seem less curious than she felt.

"Yeah," Jane continued. "Polly had been pushing her luck for a long time – way before you got here. You just happened to hear it all kicking off. She's been carted off to somewhere else already. I don't know where. I was just told to arrange the coachman and Master Cutler took it from there."

"What did Polly do that was so bad?"

"It's a long story, but the top and tail of it is that Master really isn't one to be made a fool of. He's not an impatient man by any means but he has… hmm... he can be very particular about how he likes things to be done."

"That's understandable," Roberta said, trying to get as much information as possible from Jane. "If he knows what he wants, it could make our jobs easier because it saves us from having to guess."

"It depends what he's asking for," Jane quipped back, an air of defensiveness in her tone.

Roberta didn't know what Jane meant but she made a mental note that she would have to be cautious around her new employer. She was now under the impression that he was probably quite strict. Keen to change the subject anyway, Roberta decided to take the opportunity to learn more about Jane.

"Do you like it here?"

"It's ok," Jane replied. "It's not bad. It's the fourth place I've served. It's probably more organised here than the other places I've served but then Master Cutler is quite high up in society because of his job. I suppose to get to his level of success, one would have to be something of a perfectionist, or at least certainly close to it."

Roberta could sense that Jane's approach to being in service was probably not too different to her own. Neither of them seemed to have a burning desire to question what was asked of them. It wasn't that they lacked the intelligence to do so but certainly, emotionally, they were both of the overall mindset that the way to be comfortable in their lives was to serve and to serve well.

In some ways, Roberta considered that she would be happy to wait for an introductory meeting with her new employer. Having seen the mood he'd been in this morning, she figured that maybe it would go in her favour to keep a low profile for a while – at least until Master Cutler had hopefully calmed down. From the smallest glimpse of time in which she had been able to observe him, he struck Roberta as a man who could probably be quite intimidating.

"You'll probably be best placed in the kitchen with me for the foreseeable," said Jane. "I appreciate the help and I don't mind doing all the errands for Master Cutler until he is ready to meet you."

"That's kind. Thank you."

"My pleasure," Jane said with a smile. "I'll take his meal up to him later while you clean up in here."

It was almost as if Jane didn't want Roberta to meet Master Cutler just yet. On the one hand, Roberta found it strange but on the other, she reasoned that Jane was just being kind and trying to look out for her as the new servant.

As Roberta turned to the sideboard to start chopping some carrots, she heard the kitchen door open behind her. A cheery male voice called out.

"Helloooo! I've got some fresh vegetables from the garden. Where in the pantry would you like me to leave them?"

"Hello Albus," Jane's voice seemed higher as she greeted the young man. "This is Roberta, the new servant here. Roberta, this is Albus, the gardener."

"Nice to meet you Albus," said Roberta as she turned to see who she was talking to.

"Albus is great," Jane beamed as she tapped his muscled arms playfully. "He's always bringing us fresh stock from the garden to help with the cooking. Aren't you Alby Pie?"

Jane was clearly flirting with the gardener. It made Roberta cringe but the man himself seemed to enjoy the attention. He was taller than Jane. He grinned down at her, appreciating and welcoming her eagerness.

"Looks like you can't come for a walk with me outside at the moment," Albus sighed as he addressed Jane. "I assume it needs to be all hands on deck in here, especially after what happened with Polly."

"You heard about it then," said Jane. "It is a shame but it seems like things between her and Master Cutler became too awkward."

Raising an eyebrow, Roberta was hopeful that maybe she would find out more from this conversation.

"Silly girl," laughed Albus as he gave Jane a playful shake by her shoulders. "Her insubordination has given you more work to do and now you can't come and help me outside."

"Chin up," laughed Jane. "Maybe later, you never know."

As Jane winked at Albus, Roberta was certain that there was something going on between the two of them. *So be it*, she thought to herself. Although she was still none the wiser about her new employer, she was starting to see quite a few different sides to Jane. It struck Roberta that perhaps Jane had the propensity to be quite fickle. She was certainly a flirt and knew how and when to turn on the charm as it suited her.

"Well," said Albus jovially. "If my favourite girl has to stay here in the kitchen, I'd better get back to it. I'll see you ladies later, weather depending of course."

Roberta wasn't quite sure what Albus was on about but before she'd had the chance to ask, the gardener closed the conversation of his own accord.

"Nice to meet you, Roberta."

And after playfully tapping Jane on the tip of her nose with his forefinger, he was gone.

Chapter Six

The afternoon had passed quietly. Roberta and Jane were running out of things to say to each other and so the two of them contentedly worked into the evening. They did some dusting and some organising of the pantry prior to attending to the evening's meal once it had all boiled together nicely. The inviting smell of rabbit stew filled the whole kitchen. It reminded Roberta of how hungry she was. An apple for breakfast hadn't helped her stave off the hunger that she had accrued from travelling the day before.

Just as Jane was getting everything ready to take to Master Cutler, there was a knock at the door. Albus was back.

Jane put the ladle down carefully, smiling at Albus as she did so.

"You don't half pick your moments, you know."

"Don't pretend you're not pleased to see me," Albus said with a shrug.

"Yeah, yeah, you're a smart one you," she giggled playfully before turning towards Roberta. "I'm popping out for a bit. I won't be long. Don't let the stew get cold and be sure to keep stirring it. Make sure it doesn't stick."

Before Roberta could even think to protest, Jane bounded out of the kitchen to be with Albus, slamming the door behind her as she went.

Roberta felt uncomfortable. She trusted that Jane wouldn't be long but she was surprised at how willingly she had dropped what she was doing in order to attend to something of her own interest. It seemed a shame to have the dinner so close to being served only to abandon the task at the last minute for something that was surely less important.

Oh well, Roberta thought. *At least it won't be long until Master Cutler is served his meal.*

As if right on cue, Roberta became convinced that she could hear a grandfather clock chiming somewhere else in the building. She figured that even if she had imagined it, it must be getting late. It was dark outside and probably cold too.

Not wanting to risk being held accountable for any errors on her first day, Roberta decided that it would be best if she could call Jane back into the kitchen to get on with serving the master's dinner. When she opened the door to call her though, there was nobody there. Roberta could only assume that Jane had gone off somewhere with Albus and had lost track of time in doing so.

Roberta was convinced that Jane was running the risk of delaying the dinner service to the point that one or both of them would cause disappointment. After seeing the mood that Master Cutler had been in earlier that day, Roberta couldn't justify delaying the meal any longer and so she took it upon herself to take the stew off the heat. She was determined to take the meal up to her new employer herself.

Chapter Seven

As Roberta carefully wheeled the trolley with the meal on down the corridor towards the study, she had a moment of anxiety when she realised that Master Cutler probably wasn't one to dine in that same room where she had first encountered him earlier that day.

Seeing as she was now near the study, Roberta decided to check in there anyway, just in case. But no, Master Cutler wasn't there.

Due to how challenging it would be to manoeuvre the service trolley through the vast corridors of the large house, Roberta decided that it would be easier for her to knock on the doors of all the rooms nearby in the hope that Master Cutler would be in one of them. That way, she figured, she would be able to bring his meal to him at lightening speed rather than pushing the trolley to every room.

Big mistake! Roberta didn't know that yet though.

She ran quickly down the corridor knocking on every door and then ran straight back up towards the serving trolley. No sooner had she got there did she hear a male voice at the end of the corridor.

"Yes? Who is it? What do you want?"

It was Master Cutler. He had stepped outside into the corridor to see what the commotion was all about. Without thinking ahead, Roberta charged towards him with the trolley, causing the plates and the cutlery to clatter as she did so. It wasn't until she dug her heels into the floor to halt her speed that she found herself cringing in embarrassment; the stew was all over the surface of the trolley and although there was still plenty in the bowl, the presentation of the whole thing now looked absolutely awful. Sloppy. Lazy. Roberta cast her eyes downwards in the presence of the tall man, frustrated with herself from knowing that she could have done better.

Rather than saying anything, Master Cutler walked back into the room and motioned at Roberta to follow him. As he sat down at the table, he watched Roberta with interest.

"Sorry I'm late Master. I'm really sorry it's late. And I've made such a mess. Shit. I'm really sorry," she stammered.

"Silence please," he said in a matter-of-fact tone.

Roberta sharply inhaled, shocked at the abruptness of her employer's manner.

"Stop what you're doing," he said coldly.

As she looked up from the messy serving tray in her hands, Roberta felt her cheeks burn scarlet as the distinguished man stared at her. Taking his time, he spoke to her slowly and clearly.

"First of all, when you are in my presence, you do not swear. Is that understood?"

Roberta nodded anxiously.

"Answer me properly."

"Yes Master. Sorry Master. It won't happen again Master."

"Secondly, don't ever create such a commotion

in the corridor like that again. What on earth were you thinking?"

"I... err... I wasn't..."

"Exactly! You weren't thinking, were you?"

"No Master, I don't think I was. I'm sorry Master."

"Well. It's happened now. I expect more from my servants."

Roberta felt Master Cutler's comment cut through her like a knife. She wanted so badly to be good at her new job and so far it seemed that she had failed miserably. It hurt her to think that even though she knew she was capable of doing better, she had failed to prove it.

She felt frustrated and defeated. By this point, she was trying hard not to cry. She was desperate not to do so in front of her new employer. She feared that it would look shamefully self-indulgent, especially in view of how much she had managed to disappoint him thus far.

Master Cutler glared at Roberta from across his still-empty table.

"Your references were absolutely stellar, Roberta. Are you really behaving in a way that gives me cause to doubt their validity?"

Roberta could feel her heart thumping against her chest. She didn't know how to answer the question. She felt just as startled as the rabbit in the stew must have done upon being caught.

The Master motioned towards Roberta to place the meal on the table. He dismissed her as quickly as he thanked her for the food itself.

Just as Roberta was about to leave the room, Master Cutler demanded her attention once more.

"I can't fault the flavours but this stew is stone cold," he said flatly. "Today has been a disappointment and your poor service has compounded matters further. It's unacceptable. I expect better – much better – next time."

Once properly dismissed and out of the room, Roberta pushed the serving trolley with aggressive desperation. She wanted to get as far away from the room as possible, willing herself not to burst into tears within earshot of the man who she had so drastically let down. The feeling burned in the pit of her stomach, its harshness exacerbated by the fact that all she had wanted to do was please him.

Chapter Eight

Roberta sadly wheeled the trolley into the kitchen. She was relieved to notice that Jane wasn't around. Part of her needed to be alone. She still felt tearful and didn't want anyone to see her like this – not Master Cutler and not her colleagues either. She felt that to show weakness would be to alienate herself from the people who she was still trying to make a good impression on.

Resting her elbows upon a large chopping board, Roberta slunk down and planted her forehead on her arms. Much to her frustration, she began to sob. It had all been too much. She had been so good at her old job. She knew the ropes and had maintained a good rapport with her employers and the other servants. She was beginning to miss how easy it had been there. Having started there when she was fourteen, everyone had been so patient with her. They had helped her to learn and grow from her mistakes as they took her under their wing. Roberta cried for what had been and for how alone she felt in her new circumstances. She cried for how anxious she was about the unknown. She cried with exasperation at how Master Cutler's first impression of her must have been an awful one. She wondered if she would ever be able to turn things around.

Just as Roberta was starting to pull herself together, she felt grateful for the fact that Jane was still away from the kitchen. She admitted to herself that she had probably needed a good cry. It had been a tense couple of weeks for her all round. With tears still in her eyes though, she jumped to attention as Jane burst through the door looking somewhat flustered and amused.

It was clear that Jane had lost track of the time and had enjoyed herself whilst doing so. She didn't look too worried – or even aware – of how long she had been away from her duties. There was a nonchalance about her that Roberta was beginning to find difficult. Despite this, it was hard for her to be completely annoyed at Jane, who had an endearing cheekiness about her at times.

"It's cold out there," Jane said hastily. "He's a

fun one, that Albus. Anyway, I… What's wrong with you? Have you been crying?"

Roberta rubbed her sleeve across her eyes in a feeble attempt to make it look like she was tired or had allergies. It was no use though. She really didn't want to let on to Jane that she was struggling so much, especially after what had just happened with Master Cutler.

It had been so long since someone had asked Roberta if she felt ok and, even if Jane's question may have been somewhat insincere, it made her start crying again. Instinctively, Jane ran up to her and took her in her arms. This made Roberta cry even harder.

"Shhh… shh…." Jane soothed. "Whatever it is, I'm sure it will come to nothing. Do you want to talk about it?"

Roberta really didn't want to talk about it at all. She was embarrassed and ashamed about what had just happened. All of it. She knew though that she needed to explain it to Jane. If Jane went to serve another meal to Master Cutler in the mood that he was in, she could end up bearing the brunt of things and Roberta didn't want that to happen because that wouldn't be fair at all.

Even though Jane had perhaps been lapse – and even a bit selfish – in wandering off for so long, Roberta didn't want to drop her in it. Even if Jane could be a bit dippy at times, she seemed nice enough that Roberta didn't want to get her into trouble.

"I've messed up really badly," said Roberta, desperately searching Jane's eyes for approval.

"Don't be silly. You haven't done anything."

"No really, I have. That's the problem."

"But you've been here in the kitchen the whole time."

"I haven't though. I'm so sorry."

"What are you on about?" said Jane, trying to make sense of what Roberta was clearly struggling to say.

Roberta took a deep breath, preparing to reveal what had happened. She felt that she owed Jane an explanation.

"Ok," she said. "Well, you were gone for quite a while and having seen the mood that Master

Cutler was in earlier today, I didn't want to take the risk of allowing him to be disappointed further. I tried to find you to remind you to take his meal up. But you were nowhere to be seen. So I took it upon myself to present his meal to him. But I messed the whole thing up. Really badly."

"Why did you do that? I said I wouldn't be long. I wasn't was I?" Jane sounded confused more than anything.

"Well," Roberta said hesitantly. "Yes."

Jane suddenly felt confronted by a mixture of emotions. She didn't know whether to be annoyed at herself for having lost track of the time when enjoying a moment with Albus, or whether to be insulted by the fact that Roberta had disregarded her on her first day. Not only that, but it was Roberta's incompetency that would reflect badly on both of them.

"Couldn't you have waited?" asked Jane.

She took a step back from Roberta, suddenly less trusting of her new colleague and cautious of whether or not to comfort her anymore.

"I tried, I really did try," Roberta pleaded. "But, you know, the stew was starting to look like it really needed to be served and I was anxious about displeasing Master Cutler on my first day."

Jane's tone suddenly changed to one of frustration.

"So because you couldn't trust me to get everything sorted – just like I said I would – you took it upon yourself to make the situation all about you and consequently, messed things up for all of us."

"Please don't be mad at me," Roberta urged desperately. "I thought I was doing what was right for everyone."

"I'm sure you meant well," said Jane. "But you've now put us both in a position where we could be in the master's bad books. I want to be on your side, I really do, but this is now incredibly awkward."

"What should we do? Is there anything we can do to make it better?" Roberta asked, trying to be helpful and wanting to offer a practical solution.

"I really don't know," Jane said doubtfully. "But what I do know is that if this comes back on me, it's going to be really uncomfortable for both of us."

Roberta knew that even though it sounded like it, Jane wasn't making a threat. She was right.

Chapter Nine

The following day, as Jane and Roberta dusted around the corridors, Roberta worked hard to take note of the geography of the house. She was keen to get her bearings; this was especially important considering that between the two of them, they had decided that Roberta would serve Master Cutler his evening meal. A different set of servants were responsible for his breakfast so it had allowed Roberta time to calm down, and Jane some time to work out what would be best in terms of how to make things up to their employer when it came to serving his dinner.

Jane had decided that it would be best if she didn't serve Master Cutler's evening meal on the basis that if anyone was going to bear the brunt of his bad mood, it should be Roberta. After all, it was she who had charged ahead with things and not had the patience and trust to just do as she had been asked in the first place. Roberta, although nervous about seeing Master Cutler again, was in agreement with Jane. Firstly, she didn't want Jane to get in trouble but also, she figured that it would be a good opportunity to at least try to put things right after messing up so badly the first time around.

Roberta was relieved with how she and Jane had worked things out because she didn't want to fight with anyone. She didn't even cope well when there were slight tensions. It just wasn't in her nature.

Evening came along soon enough and it wasn't long before Roberta once again found herself pushing the serving trolley along the vast corridors of the house as she headed towards Master Cutler's dining room. She felt confident that she knew where she was going this time. She was especially careful with the trolley to ensure that the meal wasn't spilt all over it like last time. She wanted to please. She *needed* to please.

As she approached the door of the dining room, Roberta felt less in control about everything. She steeled herself to be bold and effective. She knew that all she needed to do was serve the meal well. She had already decided that she wanted to apologise for the day before. She knew that whether or not she would be able to though, would depend very much on how things went once she was in the room and in the presence of Master Cutler.

She knocked on the door determinedly and it wasn't long after that she was told to come in. In front of her was Master Cutler sat waiting for his meal.

"Good evening Master," Roberta said clearly, keen to come across as chirpy and helpful, just like how Jane probably would.

"Good evening. You're early," he replied.

Roberta giggled nervously, unsure as to whether he was complaining or merely making a polite observation. To be on the safe side, she opted to serve the meal silently. She knew her place and she knew that her opinions and feelings didn't matter in the grand scheme of things. All she needed to do was serve the meal and serve it well.

It was Master Cutler who broke the uncomfortable silence.

"It smells good. I'm looking forward to this."

Although at times Roberta wished she wasn't so keen to be praised, she couldn't help but feel happy that she had done something right. It was small, but to her, it was something. Anxiously taking the opportunity to break the ice – even whilst knowing that it wasn't really her place to – she spoke carefully.

"I'm really sorry about yesterday Master, *really* sorry. I know it's not my place to say so but I want so much for you to know that it was a mistake on my part and that I promise such a thing will never happen again."

"Accidents happen," said Master Cutler, sensing her reluctance. "I trust that it won't happen again."

"Thank you for trusting me Master – and for giving me a chance. I appreciate it," Roberta said humbly.

It was important to Master Cutler that anyone who served him had confidence. He took great pride in helping his servants reach their full potential. He was one to command respect, dignity and order at all times but it wasn't to the extent that he was cold and unfeeling. He had the self-awareness to know that he could come across as such. He felt that sometimes it was right for him to be that way with his servants, but certainly not always.

"About the other morning…" he said.

Surprised that he wanted to engage, Roberta gave him her full attention.

"I want you to know that Polly was dismissed because there were problems. She didn't like being told what to do and I had to let her go. What use is a servant who won't do as they're told?!"

Roberta wrung her hands and laughed nervously. She couldn't tell if she was being asked a question where an answer was expected of her, or whether she was simply to nod and smile and her employer's musings.

Sensing Roberta's discomfort, Master Cutler asked her a question.

"Do you like being told what to do?"

"I suppose I do. It makes life easier that way," Roberta replied honestly.

"But do you *like* being told what to do?"

"I um… I'm not sure what you mean."

Pushing his chair back and standing pointedly, Master Cutler walked towards Roberta from behind the table. It was so unexpected to her that her feet felt frozen solid to the very spot upon which she stood.

"I'll ask you again," he said as he put his hands on her shoulders and put his face closer to hers. "Do you *like* being told what to do?"

Roberta didn't know what to say. She felt her cheeks burning crimson and she didn't know where to look, even though the man's eyes were glaring right into hers. She could feel the warmth of his breath on her face. He was so close that she was taken aback not only by how forward he was being, but by his soulful expression and the low growl in his voice. Darting her eyes towards the floor, she was desperate to avoid his question.

Putting his mouth right next to her ear, he instructed her clearly.

"I think you'd better go and face the wall and think about your answer, don't you?"

Roberta was so confused that she could only squeak out her reply.

"Yes Master."

Once facing the wall, Roberta could hear her employer settling down at the table. She could hear the cutlery against the plate as he began to eat.

"Put your hands on your head," he called across to her.

Roberta could hear that he was eating his meal at a tormentingly slow pace. She could tell that he was enjoying himself. *Is he angry at me and trying to make it clear, or is this just in his nature?* she wondered.

Something about her predicament caused Roberta's mind to drift between phases of being hyper alert to extremely calm and accepting of the situation. The pattern on the wallpaper became very familiar to her as her employer took his time to enjoy the meal – either that or he was deliberately trying to prolong her discomfort.

"Thank you for the meal," said Master Cutler, a satisfied lilt in his voice. "You may go now."

Roberta was dreading turning around and couldn't bear the thought of making eye contact with the man who had just made her feel chronically uncomfortable. And so in trusting that she had been excused, in a flurry of embarrassment she quickly put everything from the table back onto the trolley. The whole thing rattled as she frantically made a dash to leave the room. She looked clumsy and degraded, much to the pleasure of Master Cutler who sat watching her with great amusement.

Chapter Ten

Several days passed by in a blur. Roberta was so dumbfounded by what had happened with Master Cutler that night that she had managed to find ways to avoid him. She had persuaded Jane to serve the meal to him over the last few days, having urged her that it was a good chance for both of them to get back in their employer's good books after the poor service they had given that memorable night.

Roberta always found it strange how Jane never came back looking confused, worried or flustered from any of her own interactions with Master Cutler. *Maybe Jane likes it, or maybe she's used to it and is better at taking it in her stride*, Roberta thought to herself.

Eventually though, curiosity got the better of her and so one day whilst they were scrubbing the dirty linen, she asked Jane outright.

"How do you deal with it?"

"I just wring it out as often as my hands can take and try not to get my garments so soiled in the first place."

"No, not the linen," Roberta sighed. "You know, the way he is with us."

"Who?" Jane asked, baffled.

"Doesn't he make you uncomfortable: Master Cutler?"

"No. Why would he? What is there to feel uncomfortable about?" Jane said with a raised eyebrow.

"You know, when he makes you face the wall and put your hands on your head."

Roberta hadn't wanted to be so candid with Jane but she was keen to know if Master Cutler treated all of his servants in such a way.

"Ah," Jane said with a knowing smile. "I see what you mean now."

"How do you handle it?"

"I don't," Jane said bluntly. "That is to say, it's

never been a problem for me because Master Cutler has never taken to me in that way. But I know it does happen."

"Does it?!" exclaimed Roberta, genuinely surprised that Jane seemed so carefree about the whole thing.

"You know the thing with Polly… well… it wasn't just about her insubordination," Jane explained. "Yes, she did answer back and no, she didn't like being told what to do, but there was more to it than that."

"Oh?"

"Basically, Master Cutler used to enjoy exerting his power over her until one day she snapped. She went on strike and as well as gossiping to the rest of us, she tried to persuade us all to go on strike. When word got back about it to Master Cutler, his only option was to send her away. I suppose she was only standing up for herself but what was she to do?"

"What would you have done in her shoes?" Roberta asked.

"Honestly?" said Jane. "I'd have taken advantage

of it, I suppose. A few extra days off, a few extra home comforts here and there perhaps. I recommend that you do the same. Unless you hate it enough to follow in Polly's footsteps and behave in a way that would get you banished."

Everything that Jane was saying was making Roberta's mind whirl. The more she found out, the more she couldn't relate to the hatred that Polly had had for the situation. Even Jane's indifference was difficult for Roberta to relate to. When Master Cutler had been telling Roberta what to do, in some ways, it had made her feel safe and comforted. In those moments, she didn't have to think for herself. She was free from her own busy mind and she was making someone happy by doing things that challenged her but were not too much trouble in the grand scheme of things.

"Snap out of it will you!" Jane called to Roberta. "You can try and avoid him if you like but you can't get away with that forever. You'll have to just go along with it and not let it bother you."

But that's the problem, Roberta thought to herself. A part of her was curious about what had happened, even though she was startled by it and almost offended in some ways.

With Roberta having let on to Jane what had happened, Jane was determined not to let her hide from their employer. She wasn't prepared to cover for someone who didn't have the guts to face up to their responsibilities.

"You can take his meal to him tonight. I think it will be good for you," Jane advised. "Have a think about what you want to get out of the situation – I would."

Roberta figured that she and Jane were on drastically different pages when it came to the problem in hand; where Jane saw an opportunity, Roberta's perception of things was more emotional.

There was no use in arguing with Jane. Besides, she had already helped Roberta to avoid Master Cutler for a good few days now and it wasn't fair to expect her to do the same every night.

Rubbing the wet garment over the washboard with frustration, Roberta knew that she would have to see Master Cutler in a matter of mere hours.

Chapter Eleven

Dinner time came around soon enough. Roberta had already decided that she was going to get it over and done with as quickly as she could. She promised herself that as soon as she had served Master Cutler his meal, she would leave the room promptly and professionally.

There was a part of her that was curious to see what would happen if she stayed in the room with him. Overall though, she had already decided that he was probably just testing the waters that day when he had asked her to stand and face the wall. *Yes, that must be it*, Roberta thought to herself. *He must have just been checking that I was willing to comply with his orders – especially seeing as he'd had to let another servant go for insubordination.*

Tonight's meal was warm bread and dripping. Roberta felt confident that she would be able to serve such a meal to Master Cutler quickly enough without any awkwardness. Bracing herself, she knocked on the dining room door.

"Come in," he called.

It was as if he had been expecting her at that very moment. Roberta felt uncomfortable as soon as she stepped into the room.

Master Cutler wouldn't stop staring at her. He watched her every little move in great detail – from how she picked up the cutlery to how she bent down to pick up the plate of warm bread.

The silence of the room could have been cut with a knife. Master Cutler's eyes were almost bug-like as he followed Roberta's every move as she began to place everything on the table.

He didn't say thank you to Roberta and so in not wanting to overstep any boundaries, she quickly smiled at him. She swiftly grabbed hold of the serving trolley and made her way back towards the corridor. The room was so quiet that the sound of every one of her footsteps was more noticeable than they would usually be. A loud demanding voice cut through the silence.

"Did I say you could leave?"

"Oh... no... sorry Master. Did you want me to..."

"Silence," he commanded frankly. "I don't want to hear another word from you. You should know what is expected of you this time."

Roberta couldn't believe what she was hearing. Assuming she knew what Master Cutler meant, in a questioning motion she pointed to the wall – the same wall she had stood facing with her hands on her head the last time she had served dinner.

Smiling almost sadistically, Master Cutler simply nodded and pointed to the wall to clarify what it was that he expected Roberta to do.

As anxious and as uncomfortable as she felt in that moment, following Master Cutler's demand felt very natural and very logical to Roberta. To many other servants, the instruction would have probably felt futile and infuriating, but to Roberta – although there was an element of it that felt degrading – there was a part of her that was happy to oblige in the knowledge that even if it was a trivial instruction, it was what the man wanted.

Studying the patterns on the wallpaper again, she listened as Master Cutler finished his meal. As before, he took his time and seemed to be savouring it. Roberta almost wished that she could turn around to see him – at least to be given a clue as to what his motives were. But no, she knew instinctively that she needed to keep her eyes on the wall. Besides, it could be mortifying to have to make eye contact with the man who had so much power over her.

Roberta's heart started pounding as she heard Master Cutler's footsteps approaching her slowly from behind. Like a predator toying with his prey, he seemed to be enjoying every moment of this.

As soon as he was right behind her, he put his mouth right next to her ear and in a quiet voice, spoke almost menacingly.

"Thank you for dinner. You may go now."

It took Roberta a moment to register the instruction. *What a strange order considering the tension in the air! Has he really enjoyed just watching me stand here uncomfortably?!* she wondered to herself.

With her lips pursed and her eyes downcast, Roberta turned to grab the serving trolley. She was so embarrassed that she almost forgot to collect the plates from the table. As she rushed to do so, Master Cutler cleared his throat.

"Look at me," he said as he stood at the other side of the table.

Roberta complied. Her cheeks were on fire.

"You are to meet me in the sitting room tomorrow morning," he continued. "Ten o'clock sharp. Don't be late. I have a very particular errand that I need you to run."

"Yes Master, thank you Master," Roberta stammered as she felt her heart pounding so hard she believed it was going to burst.

Her feet were once again frozen to the spot upon which she stood. It wasn't until her employer told her she was dismissed that Roberta jumped to it and fled from the room with the trolley clattering as haphazardly as her nerves.

74

Chapter Twelve

Roberta had yet another sleepless night as she stayed awake worrying. By the morning, she found it difficult to concentrate on anything and her thoughts were all over the place. So much so that she had to tell herself that whatever it was Master Cutler had in store for her, there was nothing she could do about it. Strangely enough, she took a lot of comfort in that.

She took extra care to make sure she would look presentable. Not a strand of hair was left to chance as she tied it up neatly on top of her head. She knew that Master Cutler's standards were exacting and she wanted to do everything she possibly could to get things right.

The walk from the servant's bedroom to Master Cutler's sitting room was a long one. Even though she had set off early through not wanting to be late, Roberta found herself walking slowly towards whatever it was that was waiting for her. She wanted to take some time to calm her nerves in the hope that upon coming face to face with the man who clearly got a kick out of telling her what to do, she would at least remain dignified rather than flustered.

She didn't need to knock on the door. It was already open.

"Come in," Master Cutler said cheerfully.

He somehow seemed less intense than when Roberta had last seen him. All the same though, she felt her heart skip a beat when he closed the door behind them. With just the two of them in the room, the way in which he could make demands of her sent her head whirling.

He got quickly to the point.

"You see that chimney over there?"

"Yes Master."

"I want you to go up it and give it a good clean. It's been very sooty for a while now."

"Of course Master."

Roberta set about the room looking for a cloth and a bucket of water. She assumed that such things would be in a cupboard nearby. Feeling concerned that she was wasting Master Cutler's time in failing to find the tools she needed for the job, as reluctant as she felt to speak up, she took it upon herself to ask him a question.

"Please may I be excused to get a bucket of water and a cloth?"

Master Cutler laughed.

"You will be cleaning the chimney with your hands – and only your hands. No more. No less," he said with a smirk.

Roberta didn't have the heart to argue. It seemed strange to her that anyone would want a job doing whilst not permitting someone to use the right tools for it.

Master Cutler took great delight in observing Roberta's very evident confusion at the situation. He relished the thought of what he could enjoy at her expense.

"Your hands," he said to Roberta as he took both of hers in his. "I want them covered in soot. I want them soiled. I want to watch you work."

Roberta gasped as he gave her hands a tight squeeze.

"You do like working for me, don't you?" he asked almost mockingly.

"Yes Master," Roberta replied, afraid to upset him. "Thank you Master."

"Good," he said as he released her hands. "I'm going to stay here throughout."

It was clear to Roberta that Master Cutler enjoyed toying with her. For no other reason would anyone wish to watch somebody work, least of all on a task like cleaning the chimney.

***

Being inside the chimney was awful. It looked to Roberta like it hadn't been cleaned in a long time. Cynically, she even laughed quietly to herself at the idea that maybe Master Cutler had been saving it for her. *How funny it would be*, she thought, *if this man has been waiting for someone like me – someone who he can boss around for the fun of it*. The absurdity of the situation made Roberta start laughing to herself once again but she then caught her breath wrong. As a result, she started to choke and madly scrambled down the chimney as quickly as she could.

Once down on the hearth, after catching her breath, she wiped her blackened arm across her forehead.

She looked up and could hardly believe what she was seeing. Sat on the chair and watching her intently, although fully dressed, her employer was pleasuring himself.

Still on the floor and covered in soot, it was now as clear as day to Roberta: Master Cutler was enjoying her servitude – and indeed her discomfort – to the ultimate extent.

Chapter Thirteen

Over the months, Roberta's explicit encounters with Master Cutler continued. She had grown to enjoy it, *crave* it even. She was very aware of how much lust she had for him. There was even a part of her that wanted to get to know the man behind the veneer of dominance with which he addressed her. She had grown to care about him. There had been times where, when he had grabbed her hands, she had felt jolts of electricity run all the way through her entire being.

Jane was aware of the goings-on and was completely unsurprised by it all. She had been in service to Master Cutler for long enough that she knew the drill.

One day, when washing the dirty linen with Roberta, Jane offered her some frank advice.

"I wouldn't recommend getting too close to him."

"Why not?" Roberta asked naively. "And anyway, who says that I'm getting close to him?"

"Come on," said Jane. "It's obvious. You have a spring in your step every time you go to serve him and even the very mention of his name sometimes makes your voice go a little higher than it usually would."

"Really?" Roberta asked, genuinely surprised.

"Yes. Look, I've seen this before and I just don't want you to get hurt. Imagine if things got complicated or if they came to a head to the point that you had to be sent away to work somewhere else. It happened to Polly."

"But you said that Polly was rebellious."

"She was. But maybe something made her snap. Maybe she enjoyed being subordinate to Master Cutler at first, but then when she wanted something from him that he wasn't willing to give, things got turbulent."

"Like what? If she was subordinate to him at any point, why would she have suddenly rebelled?"

"Love," Jane said bluntly. "Look, it was probably

the case that Polly didn't fall for him. She is a very different woman to what you are. I'm just saying though, look after yourself. What good would it be to you if you got too close to him?"

Roberta's mind raced as she tried to take in everything that Jane was saying. Jane had made a good point and now Roberta was feeling confused. *Am I getting exceptional feelings for him?* she asked herself. And the thing that really worried her is that, upon thinking about it, she figured that it was a very plausible likelihood.

"Maybe I've said too much," Jane said, not wanting to worry Roberta. "You do you. Just be sure to look out for number one when all is said and done."

Jane's intelligence was admirable. Even as a servant, she had the self-awareness to recognise the power of staying in touch with a sense of self-interest. Roberta was impressed by it because – unlike Jane – although she certainly had the propensity to be self-serving on an instinctive level, it was often the case that she found herself being concerned about others before she would stop to spare a thought for herself.

Roberta was due to see Master Cutler that day.

She spent the rest of the afternoon in something of a daze, wondering to herself whether she should ask him outright what his intentions were. But why? Why should she ask him to justify himself? Surely his enjoyment of her was simply a matter of pure hedonism. If that was the case, then why would any other emotions – or indeed concerns regarding commitment or loyalty – come into it? Roberta sighed, confused and frustrated. Besides, she told herself, what was the point in trying to analyse how Master Cutler felt about her, or indeed how she felt about him? She would never be more than a servant to him; why would it make sense for her to ask him a question where any answer he could give would be meaningless anyway. More to the point, Roberta thought, she wouldn't dare to ask him an unsolicited question, least of all one of such a personal nature. As close as she felt to him in those moments where he took his pleasure from her, there had never been an instance in which she had spoken out of turn. It was always a case of *yes Master, no Master, thank you Master* or *sorry Master.*

Master Cutler would often take his pleasure from telling Roberta off for any transgression that he deemed meaningful enough to pull her up on. On one occasion, one of the carrots in the meal she served him had tasted a bit off. Consequently, he ordered her to go into the garden and dig up some fresh vegetables. As with when he had sent her up the chimney with no tools for the job, he did the same when ordering her to get to work in the garden. Luckily for Roberta, Albus wasn't around to bear witness, at least, she hoped he wasn't. She had no chance of knowing because Master Cutler stood right over her the whole time, watching her dig in the ground with her bare hands. She had needed to keep stopping to relieve herself of the discomfort when dirt got under her fingernails. There were also times where she had to alternate between leaning on one hand whilst digging with the other – anything to get the job done. Master Cutler had gently but firmly pressed her hand closest to him into the dirt with his boot. It had made her gasp – not just in shock, but in some kind of pleasure.

Shaking her head from the enjoyment of her daydream, Roberta took a moment to remind herself of who she was. She was Master Cutler's servant. Nothing more. No matter what questions the conversation with Jane had put in her head, it was not her place to voice them, least of all to him. He didn't owe his servants anything, and in a way, to Roberta, there was a lot of beauty, relief and comfort in that. She liked knowing what to expect and she thrived on consistency. She couldn't relate to why anyone would ever want to make life more complicated.

Chapter Fourteen

"I've got a little surprise for you," Master Cutler told Roberta after she had served him his meal that evening.

Standing still behind the serving trolley with no idea of what to expect, Roberta watched as he rummaged around at the back of the room. It wasn't long before he came back holding a black evening gown.

Roberta couldn't understand it. Was such a garment really for her? Why?

Master Cutler laughed at her confused expression. He *wanted* to shock her. He *wanted* to see her put in a situation outside of her comfort zone. He wanted her to grow, even if the means by which he intended to orchestrate that would cause her some discomfort and perhaps some humiliation.

"You're going to wear this outfit when you come with me to a ball tonight. But know this…" he said as he stepped closer to Roberta with a low growl in his voice. "You are *not* to shame me by letting on to the people there that you are my servant. They must not be allowed to know that under any circumstances. Do you understand?"

Roberta hesitated, struggling to take it all in.

"I said," he growled as he put his face closer to hers. "Do you understand?"

"Yes Master, I think so."

"What do you mean you *think so*? You *know so*. You are going to come with me to the ball. Nobody needs to know who you really are. I just want you to attend with me. I want to show you something new."

Handing the dress to Roberta, he smiled at her in a way that she found almost reassuring. As challenged as she felt in that moment, she was starting to see a side to him that was kind and nurturing.

Swallowing back a lump in her throat, Roberta desperately wanted to look into his eyes. She wouldn't allow herself to do so though. She didn't want to overstep the mark. She felt that perhaps Master Cutler was trying to test her. Maybe he wanted to see if she would try to push boundaries when presented with the opportunity. On the other hand, Roberta thought to herself, maybe she was over-thinking things again and just needed to revel in the calm that she often felt when simply doing what she was told to do by this enchanting man.

"Thank you Master," said Roberta, half expecting to be told to undress in front of him.

"I will leave the room while you get ready," he said with a smile.

As much as he enjoyed putting his servant in uncomfortable and challenging situations, he didn't want to be so crass as to demand that she undress in front of him. He wanted to keep some distance. He wanted to keep some mystique. He knew that he could reduce Roberta to tears if he really wanted to and to him, the thought of that was far more intoxicating than the prospect of seeing her naked. To see her naked, that would be far too easy. It gave him far more of a thrill to dominate her in ways that were more obscure.

Once in the room alone, Roberta took a moment to observe the dress. It had long sleeves and looked like it would cover her ankles once it was on. The top of it was cut to show all of the wearer's décolleté. Roberta had never worn a dress like this before. She was grateful for the fact that of all the design features, at least it wouldn't be her hands or her knees that would be exposed – or indeed anywhere else on her person that risked communicating the fact that she was a mere servant, with marks and calluses in all the places that gave it away.

Roberta had never worn anything that sat so tightly on her skin before. As she began to pull the material over her hips, the strangeness of the whole situation washed over her once again.

She was grateful for the fact that once she had the dress on, it was only moments later that Master Cutler came back into the room.

"You look stunning," he said as he breezed towards her enthusiastically. "Just one more thing though…"

Rummaging in a nearby drawer, he soon found what he was looking for.

"Come here," he instructed.

Somewhat hesitant to know what he wanted from her, Roberta walked towards him. Wearing the dress made her feel self-conscious as the material rippled against her body – something that she was all of a sudden very aware of.

"I want you to wear this," he said as he held out a pearl necklace in front of her.

A single pearl occupied every part of the necklace with the exception of the clasp. Master Cutler held the striking trinket in an outstretched position, preparing to fasten it around Roberta's slender neck. As he bent forward to place it against her skin, she felt a surge of emotion charge through her. There was something about the way he gave her his attention that really touched a nerve. Not only that, but the fact that he had clearly put so much thought into everything made an impact on Roberta that gave her butterflies in her stomach.

"Good," he said as he stood back to admire his work. "Good… but we're not finished yet."

Roberta couldn't believe her eyes; no sooner had he dug his hand into his trouser pocket had he revealed to her a set of pearl earrings – they matched the necklace perfectly. Clipping one of them open, he took the opportunity to get close to her again. He knew that she would have never worn earrings before and was gentle as he eased it into a closed position over her earlobe.

"And now the other one," he laughed, almost cheekily as he moved across to put the other earring on.

Lost in the moment, Roberta gave a happy sigh as she caught his scent. There was something about it that she found so comforting.

Suddenly, Roberta didn't know what to do. She wanted to thank him but there were no words. She wouldn't have felt comfortable to speak to him freely and candidly anyway. In the same vein, there was a part of her that wanted to look into his eyes. She wanted to smile with him. So much, so damn much. But again, she knew that she couldn't. She felt that a mere "thank you Master" wouldn't cover things either.

And so communicating with him in the only way she knew how, she endeavoured to kneel down before him with her head bowed before saying the words.

"Thank you Master."

"You're very welcome," he said.

Chapter Fifteen

Despite the fact that Roberta spent much of it feeling drastically out of place, the ball was splendid. Master Cutler kept her close to him the whole time and so there was never any pressure for her to make conversation with the other guests. All she had to do was follow his lead. In that regard, it wasn't too different to how things usually were when she served him at his home.

Roberta managed to maintain her silence, even when he had asked her to dance. Extending his hand to welcome her onto the floor with him, he held her closer than he ever had done before as they swayed together in their own world. He was easy to dance with. He wasn't exuberant and he certainly wasn't an exhibitionist. He simply held his own; commanding his own space in the ballroom as he held Roberta in his arms with certainty.

Roberta wondered if her employer had ever taken any of the other servants to such an event before. She certainly didn't feel that it would be an appropriate question to ask him. She kept quiet all night and managed to keep her eye contact away from his, even when they were dancing. It was something that the other guests wouldn't have noticed, but the two of them both knew what it meant.

It was a beautiful evening and Roberta didn't want it to end – although she had to admit to herself that when Master Cutler had gently kissed her on the forehead while they were dancing, it confused her even though she had found it comforting.

As she lay in bed that night, Roberta couldn't stop trying to decipher what it all meant. She wanted to know if he loved her in the way that she loved him. She wanted to know what it was that he really wanted from her. She wanted to know not only what he was doing, but what he was *feeling*. She promised herself though that she would not speak out of turn to him. He was still her employer. He was still above her. Whether he was being sweet and kind or whether he was taking advantage of the power imbalance between the two of them, what did it really matter to Roberta if she was happy with the situation?

But then her mind started to wander further. What if he wanted more from her outside of her place in life? After all, he had taken her to, of all places, a ball – and a very grand one at that! It certainly wasn't normal for someone to do that with their servant.

She sighed and rolled over in bed, hoping to get some sleep. It was no use though. She noticed that Jane was fast asleep in the bed next to her but she wasn't tempted to wake her for advice, or even for company. *What good would it do to ask the opinion of someone who doesn't see the world in the same way that I do?* Roberta thought to herself.

Pulling her blanket over her for not only warmth, but comfort, Roberta closed her eyes.

96

Chapter Sixteen

The next morning – whether it was to thank her for her company at the ball or simply because he felt like it – Master Cutler gave Roberta an easier task than he could have done. As she organised some of the books on the shelves in his study, he watched her longingly.

She was determined to focus on what she had been asked to do. She had told herself that the ball shouldn't change anything.

"Last night was grand, don't you agree?"

"Yes Master," said Roberta, half in her own world.

"Maybe we could do something like that again sometime?"

Overcome with emotion, for the first time in his company, Roberta stopped attending to the task she had been set.

"Yes Master," she replied hesitantly, and not with her usual tone of conviction.

Master Cutler was always perceptive to Roberta's reactions and on this occasion, it was no different.

"Come here," he demanded.

He remained seated. With her head bowed down, Roberta walked towards him and stood in front of him as if expecting to be interrogated. She wasn't wrong.

"What on earth is the matter?" he insisted. "There was a sudden elegance about you last night but today, well, I can't put my finger on it but something seems to be wrong. What is it?"

Roberta wrung her hands anxiously inside her apron. She didn't know how to communicate what she was feeling in a way that wouldn't overstep the boundaries of her position. Sensing this, Master Cutler took it upon himself to get things in order.

"Kneel down," he said, clicking his fingers at the

spot on the floor in front of him. "I want you to tell me what's wrong. *Tell me* – and not what you think I want to hear. Tell me truthfully, what's on that mind of yours?"

Roberta started to cry. All of a sudden it felt like there was a lot at stake; her emotions and possibly even her prospects for staying in service. She was terrified that if she said the wrong thing she could be sent away.

"I want you to trust me. I want you to *tell me*," he said firmly.

"It was just so strange to be treated as equal to you," Roberta just about managed to say through sniffles and tears.

As soon as the words had left Roberta's quivering lips, she felt so relieved – lighter somehow.

Master Cutler nodded. He understood completely but he had needed to hear it from his servant, just to be sure.

"Don't you want to be treated as my equal?" he asked.

"No."

"I see…"

Worried that she had offended him, there was no stopping Roberta at this point.

"I'm so sorry to tell you this… I'm so sorry Master… but I love you." Shaking with emotion, she added quickly, "I love you – and I love serving you – but I don't want to be your equal. Please let me love you as I do. Please let me keep serving you. Please don't be offended by what I'm telling you. *Please* don't send me away."

To Roberta's utter amazement, Master Cutler was smiling. As he pulled at her hair to bring her face to meet his, there was nothing she could do to avoid meeting his gaze.

"Sending you away is the last thing I'd want to do. I want you to keep serving me. No more. No less. You get no say in whether or not I take you to another ball, or indeed anywhere else for that matter. That's not what is important here though. What matters is that you are mine. I own you and I want to keep using you. Just tell me that you feel the same."

"Yes Master," said Roberta.

Her eyes were still watering and her face was still tear-stained but this time she sparkled. She no longer radiated anxiety and apprehension.

"Wait there," he said firmly. "You don't move until I come back. Is that understood?"

"Yes Master", Roberta said calmly, trusting him wholeheartedly.

Once he was out of the room, Roberta's train of thought felt clearer than it had before. So much so that she couldn't remember the last time she had felt so free – if ever she had! She waited patiently. She felt loved, cherished and protected. Master Cutler's actions had spoken volumes in that regard.

Roberta wasn't sure how much time had passed but soon enough, Master Cutler came back into the study.

"Stay," he said playfully as he came towards her. "Now close your eyes."

As he sat down on a chair in front of her, he put something around Roberta's neck. It felt cold and heavy.

"Keep your eyes closed," he instructed. "I want you to use your hands. Feel it and tell me what you think it is."

Moving her hands towards her neck, Roberta ran them carefully around the heavy piece of jewellery that sat firmly on her décolleté. She felt certain that she knew what it was.

"What do you think it is?" he asked expectantly.

"It feels like a large chain."

"It is. And what about the focal point? Move your hands towards that."

"It feels like a padlock!"

"It is. Open your eyes."

Surely enough, when Roberta opened her eyes she could see a small padlock resting firmly above where her heart was beating excitedly in her chest.

"I have the key to that," he said. "You are in service to me and that stays around your neck because you are mine. Do you understand?"

"Yes Master, thank you Master. I understand."

Clasping the chain passionately and running her fingers over the distinctive texture of the padlock, Roberta felt the happiest she had ever felt in her life. She knew deep down that between her and Master Cutler, a meeting of souls had occurred and hopefully, this was only just the beginning.

****